Asian Giant Hornet

by Grace Hansen

INCREDIBLE INSECTS

Abdo Kids Jumbo is an Imprint of Abdo Kids
abdobooks.com

abdobooks.com

Published by Abdo Kids, a division of ABDO, P.O. Box 398166, Minneapolis, Minnesota 55439.
Copyright © 2022 by Abdo Consulting Group, Inc. International copyrights reserved in all countries.
No part of this book may be reproduced in any form without written permission from the publisher.
Abdo Kids Jumbo™ is a trademark and logo of Abdo Kids.

Printed in the United States of America, North Mankato, Minnesota.

052021

092021

 THIS BOOK CONTAINS
RECYCLED MATERIALS

Photo Credits: iStock, Minden Pictures, Shutterstock

Production Contributors: Teddy Borth, Jennie Forsberg, Grace Hansen
Design Contributors: Candice Keimig, Victoria Bates

Library of Congress Control Number: 2020947660
Publisher's Cataloging-in-Publication Data

Names: Hansen, Grace, author.
Title: Asian giant hornet / by Grace Hansen
Description: Minneapolis, Minnesota : Abdo Kids, 2022 | Series: Incredible insects | Includes online
    resources and index.
Identifiers: ISBN 9781098207342 (lib. bdg.) | ISBN 9781644945544 (pbk.) | ISBN 9781098208189
    (ebook) | ISBN 9781098208608 (Read-to-Me ebook)
Subjects: LCSH: Hornets--Juvenile literature. | Predatory insects--Juvenile literature. | Insects--Juvenile
    literature. | Insects--Behavior--Juvenile literature.
Classification: DDC 595.7--dc23

Table of Contents

Asian Giant Hornets

Asian giant hornets are **native** to the eastern and southeastern parts of Asia. They are most common in Japan. They often live near forests.

Asian giant hornets got their name for a reason. They are the largest hornets in the world!

These huge hornets have orange and black striped bodies. They have two sets of wings.

Asian giant hornet

Eastern honey bee

9

Asian giant hornets have wide, orange heads. Their eyes are the shape of teardrops. They also have powerful mandibles.

mandible

Colony Life

Asian giant hornets are social insects. They live in **colonies**.

A **colony** has three kinds of wasps. It has a queen, **workers**, and **drones**. The queen is the largest, growing more than 2 inches (5 cm) long!

The **workers** collect food and care for the nest. **Drones** have just one job. They **mate** with the queen hornet.

Colonies of Asian giant hornets live in nests. The nests are hidden. Some are underground while others are in trees.

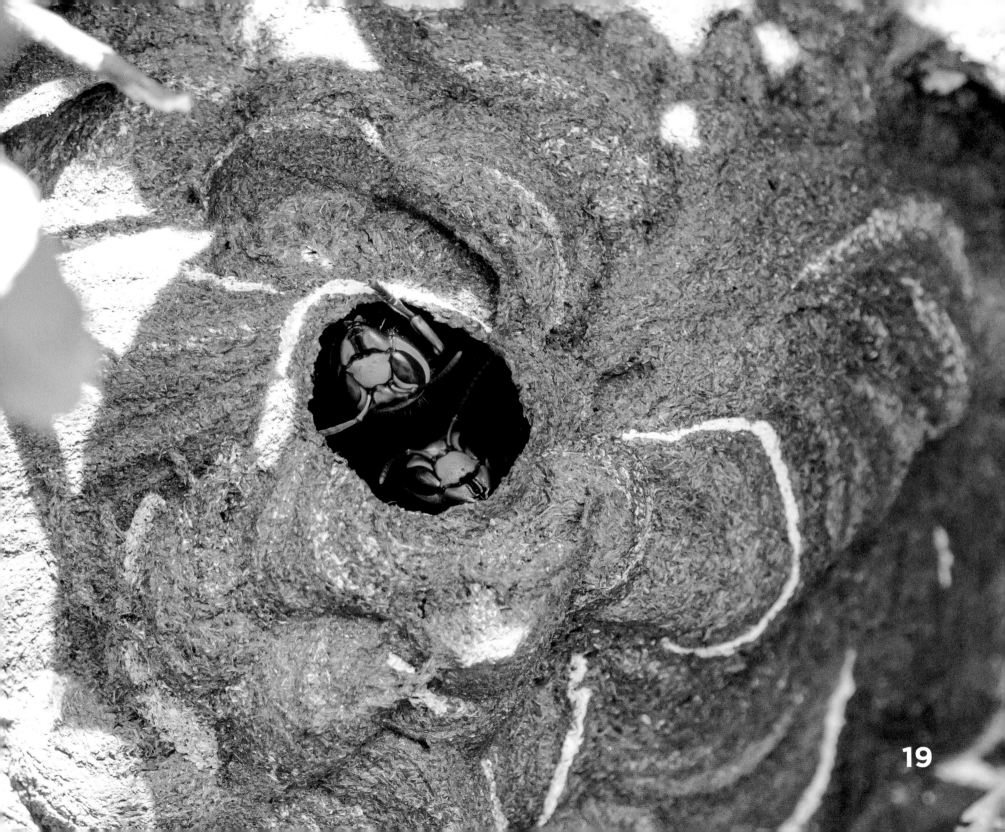

Hunting

Asian giant hornets are intense hunters. They can easily take down other large-sized insects.

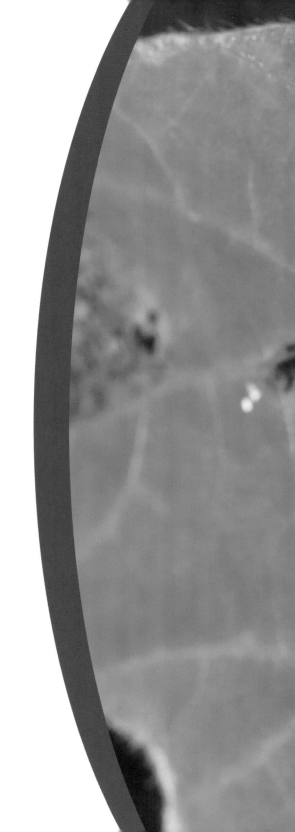

More Facts

- In the United States, Asian giant hornets are called an invasive species. This means they are not **native** to the US and can cause harm to other living things.

- Sometimes, these insects are called "murder hornets." This is because they attack beehives. They can kill 5,000 to 25,000 bees in a matter of hours.

- Queen Asian giant hornets can be around 3 times larger than honey bees.

Glossary

colony – a group of insects of the same type living together.

drone – a male hornet whose only known function is to mate with the queen.

mandible – one of the front biting mouth parts in insects.

mate – to come together to have young.

native – belonging naturally to a place.

worker – a female member of a colony of hornets that collects food and cares for the young.

Index

Abdo Kids
ONLINE
FREE! ONLINE MULTIMEDIA RESOURCES

Visit abdokids.com
to access crafts, games,
videos, and more!

Use Abdo Kids code
IAK7342
or scan this QR code!

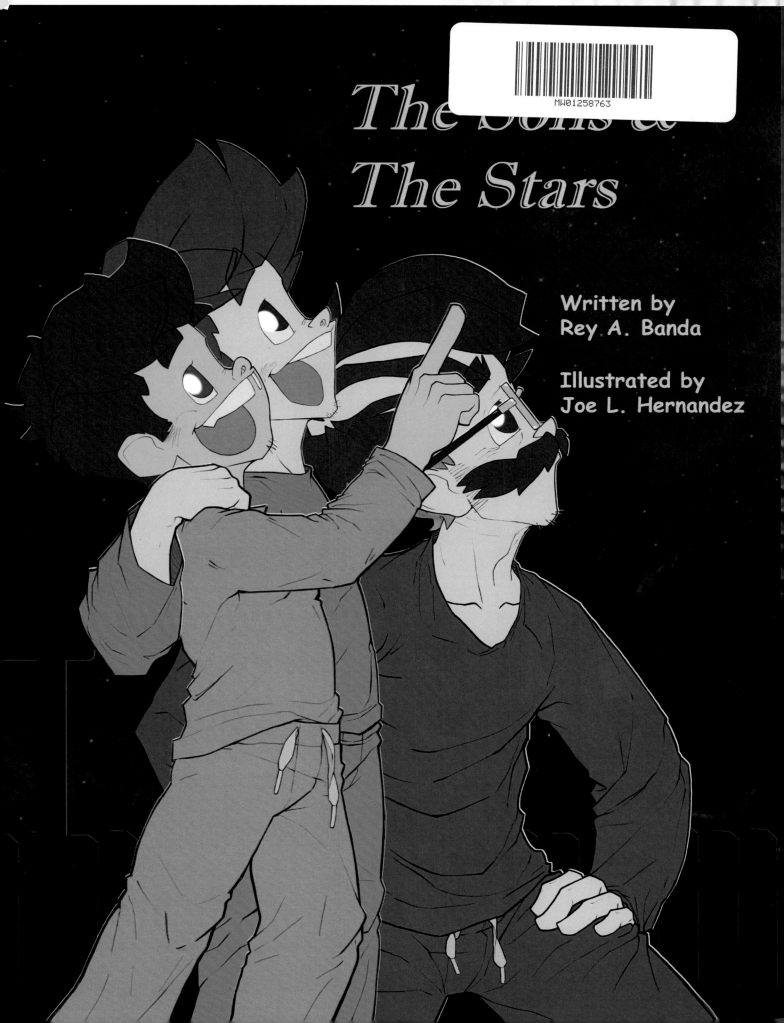

The Suns &
The Stars

Written by
Rey A. Banda

Illustrated by
Joe L. Hernandez

The Sons & The Stars
ISBN 978-0-9898090-3-0
© 2024 Rey A. Banda
Illustrations © 2024 by Joe L. Hernandez
Editing by Vanessa Castillo
Book design by Rey A. Banda
Cover editing by Randy Moses and Johnny Hernandez

NORTHOPOLIS PUBLISHING CO.

Weslaco, TX

This book is dedicated to my dad for introducing me to the vast universe of space.

There was once a father
that had two sons, John and
Ryan. The father loved to
look at the stars, especially
with his sons.

One early mornin[g]
before the sun c[omes]
up, the father w[oke]
up his sons from
their slumber.

"Hey boys, wake up! I have something really amazing to show you!" the father said.

The boys still in their pajamas, followed their dad to the backyard.

7

"Look up over there boys,"
the father said.

"Look for that 'cloudy star' in the sky," the father said.

"Oh, wow!" John said. "What is that?"

"That's a comet!"
the father said.

"I don't see it!" Ryan said to his dad. "It's right there," replied the father as he pointed to help Ryan. "Oh, I see it now!" Ryan said excitedly.

"That's Halley's Comet. It won't be around for another 76 years!" the father said.

"Wow! We will all be old men when it comes back!" Ryan exclaimed. "Well, both of you will be old men..." the father replied.

A few years later, the
father taught his sons about
the constellations in the sky.

"That one there is Ursa Major, commonly called 'The Big Dipper'," the father said as he pointed toward the northern night sky.

The father then pointed toward
the south and said, "Now if we
look at that one, we can see
'Orion'." The boys were excited to
learn about the constellations.

"Orion is named after a hunter from Greek mythology, and those three stars in the middle are known as 'Orion's Belt'," the father explained to the boys.

As the sons got a little older, the father bought them a telescope for Christmas.

The father and his sons looked at the night sky with the new telescope. "I want to see that bright star over there!" Ryan said to his dad as he pointed up.

"That's actually the planet Jupiter!" the father said as he told John to adjust the focus on the telescope.

As the boys looked through the telescope, they were amazed at how beautiful Jupiter was.

"If you loved that, then you will love this," the father said, moving the telescope in a different direction. "This is the planet Saturn."

"Oh, wow! You can actually see the rings around the planet!" John said.

One early morning, the father woke up his sons again.

28

"Another comet, Dad?" Ryan asked.

"No comet this time. Actually, we are going to lay down on the grass and look for meteors, also known as 'falling stars'." the father said.

"Okay boys, get comfortable and watch the meteors fly over us!" the father said.

The father and his sons saw many "falling stars" from the early morning up until the sun came up.

One Christmas, the sons bought their dad a very powerful telescope.

32

"Now we can see the planets and the stars even better!" Ryan said as he held the telescope.

MAX Telescope

One night, the father and sons were able to view a lunar eclipse.

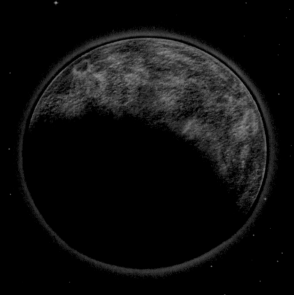

The event looked even better with their new telescope.

As time went on, the sons started their own families, but always made time to go visit and star gaze with their dad.

John and his son, Jimmy, met up with Ryan and his son, Ryder. They went over to their father's house so he could teach the grandsons about the stars.

The father told his grandsons about the stars and planets just like he did when John and Ryan were little.

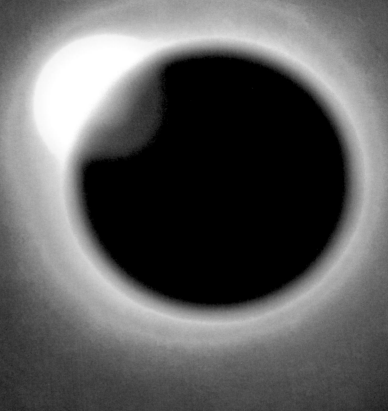

One event the whole
family was able to view
was a solar eclipse.

"Thank you Dad, for introducing us to the stars and the planets." John said.

Many years later, when John and Ryan were old and gray, they gathered together with their sons Jimmy and Ryder, along with their grandsons, Rey and Naldo.

"Look up there boys. 76 years ago, our father once showed us this comet, it's called Halley's Comet," John said.

As the younger boys were looking at the comet, Ryan and John could only think of how it was just as beautiful as when they first saw it.

"Thank you, Dad..." John and Ryan whispered.

Tears rolled down their faces.

The End

This book is based on how my dad woke my brother and I up one early morning in January 1986 to view Halley's Comet. It was a moment that I'll never forget. 1986 Halley's Comet was not the first comet that we all saw together. Comet Hale-Bopp in 1997, Comet PANSTARRS in 2013, Comet Lovejoy in 2015, Comet Catalina in 2016, Comet 45P/Honda in 2017, Comet NEOWISE in 2020, Comet Leonard in 2021, Comet ZTF in 2023, Comet 12/Brooks in 2024, and C/2023 A3 (Tsuchinshan-ATLAS) in 2024.

Rey A. Banda, a Weslaco, Texas native, is a dedicated special education teacher at a local middle school; as well as a published author of two inspirational Christmas books involving hope, love, and perseverance. His published books feature his creation of Northopolis, a magical Christmas lawn display which was featured on the national television show, "The Great Christmas Light Fight" on ABC. In addition to his Christmas books, Mr. Banda's love for his very own cat, Mr. Bean, inspired him to write his multi award-winning books titled Bean's New Home and Bean Saves the Day. Notably, Mr. Banda is also a co-founder of the nonprofit group, the "RGV Ghostbusters", who spread cheer and happiness throughout the Rio Grande Valley at various charity and nonprofit events.

Joe L. Hernandez, a Houston, Texas native, now calls the Rio Grande Valley his home. Joe is often seen as "Deadpool" at various community and charity events. Joe is also a member of the RGV Ghostbusters.